B55 062 174 8

D1437486

WITHDRAWN FROM THE ROTHERHAM PUBLIC LIBRARY

DIGGERSAURS
MISSION TO MARS

Michael Whaite

PUFFIN

Among the stars,

THE PLANET
MARS!

A giant rocky ball . . .

Where Roversaurs

complete their chores . . .

Let's go and meet them ALL!

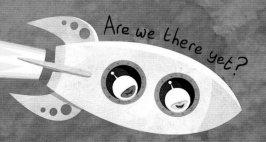

Are we there yet?

They roll **all** day

a long,

long way –

One small step for woman!

they **NEVER** stop to rest . . .

They **work** and **toil**,
collecting **soil**

to **analyse** and **test**.

MARS ROCKS!

They soar and fly, gliding high

on GIANT solar wings . . .

This one's flapping,

camera
SNAPPING,

SNAPPERSAURUS 4

Say CHEESE!

This one's **sowing**, **planting**, **growing**

vegetables and trees . . .

Construction site ahead!

with wheels as BIG as these?

They're **bold** and **brave**, exploring caves,

they **don't** have time
to **snore.**

They check the plan – a **hologram!**
The **Roversaurs**
all view it . . .

Building towers takes
SUPER POWERS!

Who on EARTH can do it?

Hmmmm...

"Help us **PLEASE!**
ROVERSAURS
to **DIGGERSAURS,**
we need your
EXPERTISE!"

Some time **later**,
in a **crater**,
see a **spaceship** land . . .

They've travelled
far through space . . .

BEEP
BEEP!
BOOP
BOOP!

To build
a **HOME**,

HOORAY!

MARTIAN BASE!!

ROCKSY

PUFFIN BOOKS

UK | USA | Canada | Ireland | Australia
India | New Zealand | South Africa

Puffin Books is part of the Penguin Random House group of companies
whose addresses can be found at global.penguinrandomhouse.com.

www.penguin.co.uk   www.puffin.co.uk   www.ladybird.co.uk

Penguin
Random House
UK

First published 2020
001

Copyright © Michael Whaite, 2020
The moral right of the author has been asserted

Printed in China
A CIP catalogue record for this book is available from the British Library

ISBN: 978-0-241-37896-0

All correspondence to:
Puffin Books, Penguin Random House Children's
One Embassy Gardens, 8 Viaduct Gardens, London SW11 7BW

MIX
Paper from
responsible sources
FSC® C018179
FSC
www.fsc.org